My Teammate Is a Hot Head

Written by **Sam Hay**

Illustrated by **Ria Maria Lee**

Disney • Hyperion
Los Angeles New York

First Hardcover Edition, April 2023
First Paperback Edition, April 2023

10 9 8 7 6 5 4 3 2 1
FAC-004510-22322

Printed in the United States

This book is set in Aptifer Slab LT Pro/Linotype
Designed by Zareen Johnson
Illustrations created in Photoshop

Library of Congress Cataloging-in-Publication Data

Names: Hay, Sam, author.
Title: My teammate is a hot head / Sam Hay.
Description: First Paperback Edition. • Los Angeles : DisneyHyperion, 2023. • Series: Camp Lil' Vills • Audience: Ages 6-8. • Audience: Grades 2-3. • Summary: "Camp Lil' Vills heats up when Hades arrives determined to win camp contests by any means necessary"—Provided by publisher.
Identifiers: LCCN 2021050354 (print) • LCCN 2021050355 (ebook) • ISBN 9781368084611 (hardcover) • ISBN 9781368057424 (paperback) • ISBN 9781368074087 (ebk)
Subjects: LCSH: Hades (Greek deity)—Juvenile fiction. • Magic—Juvenile fiction. • Camps—Juvenile fiction. • Contests—Juvenile fiction. • Teamwork (Sports)—Juvenile fiction. • CYAC: Magic—Fiction. • Camps—Fiction. • Contests—Fiction. • Teamwork (Sports)—Fiction. • Hades (Greek deity)—Fiction.
Classification: LCC PZ7.H31387385 Myg 2023 (print) • LCC PZ7.H31387385 (ebook) • DDC 813.6 [Fic]—dc23/eng/20220125
LC record available at https://lccn.loc.gov/2021050354
LC ebook record available at https://lccn.loc.gov/2021050355

Visit www.DisneyBooks.com

ATTENTION,

LILLIPUTIAN VILLAGES CAMPERS!

It's time for everyone's favorite summer tradition: the CHARMED ROPES COURSE RELAY.

- Soar through the air with your own giant griffin feather.
- Try obstacles like moving walls and the scramble web (watch out for the pink Stink Spiders!).
- Fly down the zip line, powered by your very own mind!

Winners will have their names added to the Great Treetops Trophy.

*THREE TO A TEAM. SIGN UP WITH COACH CLARY.

South Side of Camp
MUSEUM OF MYTHICAL OBJECTS
MYSTICAL MAZE
PINECONE POINT

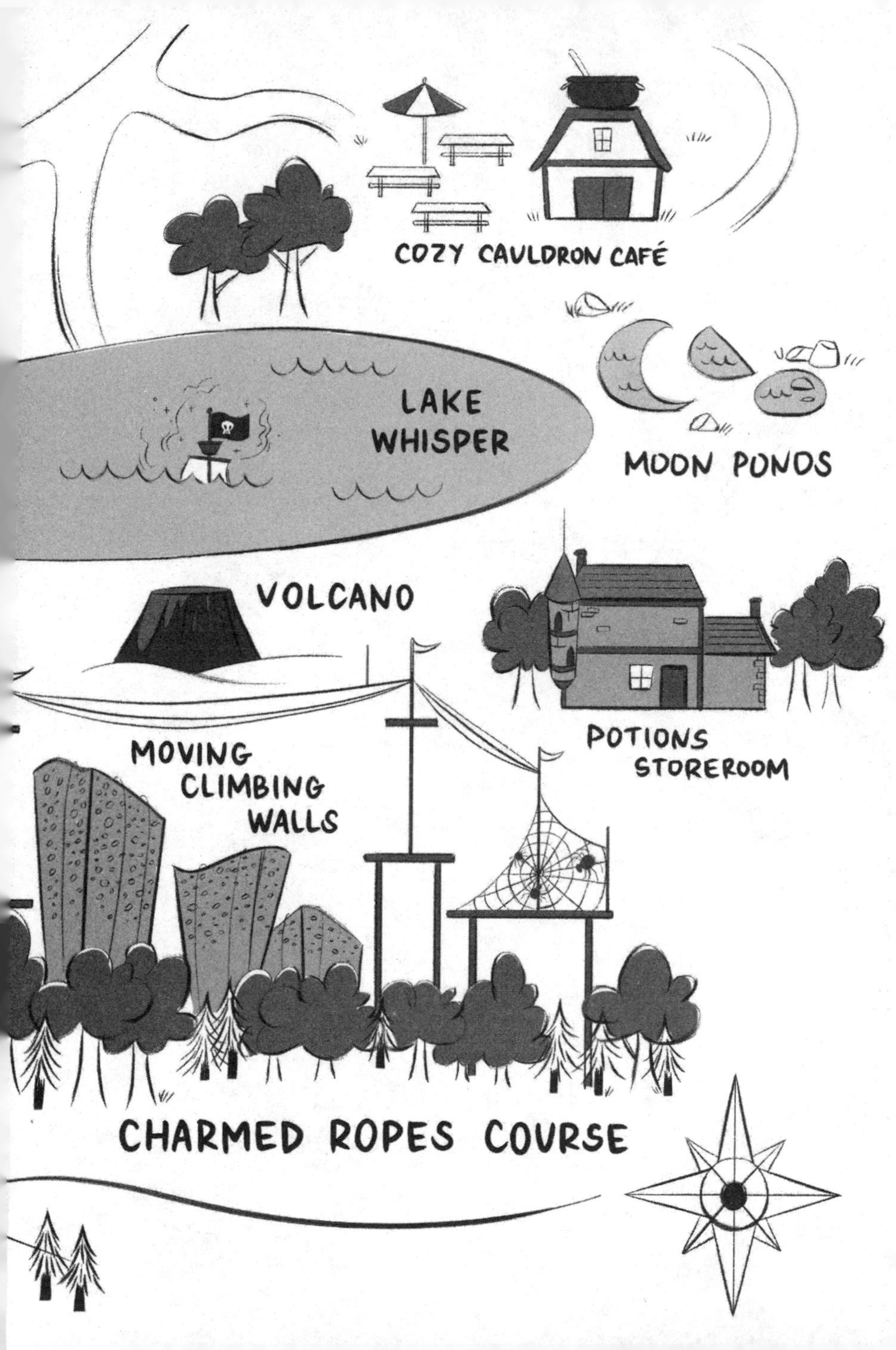
COZY CAULDRON CAFÉ
LAKE WHISPER
MOON PONDS
VOLCANO
POTIONS STOREROOM
MOVING CLIMBING WALLS
CHARMED ROPES COURSE

MY new buddy Benji picked up a giant flying feather from the pile, then glanced over the side of the platform we were standing on. "Whoa!" he breathed. "It's a long way down, Bloom."

"Don't worry," I said, wafting away a little piggy-pigeon. "As long as you say the magic words, you won't fall."

It was our third time around the Charmed Ropes Course, preparing for the team relay contest the next day, and Benji was starting to get the hang of it. But the treetops section—where you had to use a magical griffin feather to fly between the platforms—always gave him the shakes. This wasn't unusual with new campers.

Ever since my dad first opened Lilliputian Villages Summer Camp in the middle of an enchanted forest, I'd seen loads of kids crumble at the sight of the Charmed Ropes Course. For starters, it was really high up—not quite Jack and the Beanstalk level of tallness, but close! Plus, there were loads of obstacles: moving climbing walls, a spider-covered scramble web (my least favorite part), and a zip line you powered with your mind. But by the time they finished their vacation, most campers were zooming around the course like the camp's dragon squirrels.

"It's okay to be nervous," I told Benji. "The first time I did this, I tied my broomstick to my back in case the feather didn't work."

Benji looked down again, and his magical glasses flashed warning red. "According to my distance-o-meter, it's a one-hundred-and-fifty-foot drop." He gulped. "There's definitely a safety net, right?"

"Of course! And Coach Clary will catch you if you fall. She's super speedy." I pointed across to the crow's nest, where Clary was watching all the campers through her hawk-eye goggles. "And look, Hem's waiting for you. . . ."

"Hey, Benji!" My bunkmate Hem, who was the

third member of our team, waved across from the next platform.

"Okay, here goes. . . ." Benji climbed onto his feather and said the magic words. "*Bats . . . birds . . . clouds in the sky, lift this feather and make it fly*—achoo!"

Benji's sudden sneeze—caused by his magic allergy—made his feather shoot straight off the platform.

"Oh, wow!" Benji cried, clinging on to the end of the feather. "It's kind of tickly on my knees."

"You're veering right," I called. "Aim straight or you'll hit that—"

THWUMP!

Benji crashed straight into the thick, leafy branch of a giant tree, startling a mouse-owl that had been snoozing there.

"Um—I think I'm stuck," Benji called, trying to detach his sweater, which was now caught on a spiky twig.

"No problem, I'll come help," I said. "Just don't lose your feather, okay?"

But before I could launch myself off the platform, a sharp elbow nudged me out of the way and a blur of blue hair zoomed past.

"Hey!" I called. "Slow down!"

But the kid kept shooting through the air on his griffin feather, heading toward the next platform.

Unfortunately, right at that moment, Benji managed to untangle himself from the branch, and his feather rocketed toward the platform, too.

"Look out, Benji!" I called.

CLUNK!

Benji rammed right into the blue-haired kid, who let out a howl.

"Hey, make like a tree, pal!" the kid yelled, pushing Benji back into the branches.

"Hoi!" I shouted. "You can't do that!"

But the kid ignored me and carried on to the next platform.

"Er—Bloom," Benji called, trying to wriggle free. "I think I'm stuck agai—uh-oh! My feather!"

It had broken free and was now flying off without him. Benji's face turned pale as his feet dangled in the air.

"Don't move!" I picked up the largest griffin feather from the pile and climbed aboard, leaning forward just like Dad had taught me. I muttered the flying spell under my breath, and the feather took off. As I got closer, I reached out as far as I dared. "Here."

Benji hesitated. He swallowed hard, then glanced at the ground below.

"Don't look down!" I said. "Just let go of that branch and take my hand."

Slowly, he let go with one hand and stretched it out. . . .

"Gotcha!" I pulled him onto the feather. "Whoa!" I muttered as we wobbled wildly for a second. Then the feather found its balance and took off, landing us on the next platform, where Hem and the blue-haired kid were waiting.

"Oh, wow!" Hem breathed. "That was so brave, Bloom."

The kid snorted. "So much *drama.* AND you messed up my time," he added. "Now I have to start over." He pulled a piece of gum out of his mouth and stuck it to the handrail, turning to go.

"Hey, wait!" I said. "You can't leave that there. The night creatures like to play on the course, and they could get stuck."

The boy rolled his eyes. "Don't get your sandals in a spin!" But he didn't pick up his gum *or* apologize for shoving Benji as he moved away.

"Maybe next time just be more careful. You made Benji lose his feather. If Coach Clary sees you pushing other campers, she'll tell you to take a break."

The boy turned back. "A break?" His yellow eyes narrowed, and little flames shot up from the tips of his blue hair. "No one EVER tells me when to quit!" Suddenly, a large spark shot out of his hair into the branches above. Not that he noticed. He'd already jumped onto his feather and flown off.

I was about to call after him when my nose began to twitch. *Huh? What's that smell?* I glanced up. . . .

"Flashing thunderbolts," Benji said. "The tree is on fire!"

HEM let out a shriek. Benji's eyes goggled. And I felt my heart thump in my chest. Smoke was puffing around us as the flames began to spread.

"Where's Coach Clary?" Hem said, peering down at the empty crow's nest.

"It's okay," I said, trying to stop my voice from wobbling. "I'm a junior fire warden. I can put it out."

I'd practiced for this sort of emergency twice a week with the counselors ever since Dad opened the camp. But I'd never actually had to use an extinguish spell *for real*. I took a deep breath and raised my shaking hands toward the flames. *Come on, Bloom,* I told myself. *You've got this. Broomsticks crossed!* I closed my eyes and tried to picture what I was hoping to make happen; Dad often said that was the trick to getting your magic right.

"Raindrops, rivers, and creeks full of trout," I said, *"send me a cloud and put this fire out!"*

Benji sneezed, which meant the spell must have worked. I opened my eyes just as—

WHOOSH!

A gust of wind rushed past us, making the platform sway. A large fish-shaped cloud gathered overhead. It hovered next to the flames for a moment before opening its mouth like a huge fishy fire hose, and sprayed a jet of water. There was a loud *hisssss* as the water dampened the flames.

"Wizarding wands!" Benji cried. "That was awesome, Bloom."

I smiled. "I like your wipers," I said, noticing the little arms that had appeared on his lenses and were swishing the raindrops away.

Hem reached up to touch the fishy cloud. "Oh, it feels like a big sponge."

Just then, we heard a shout and Coach Clary soared up toward us.

"I'm so sorry." She panted as she landed on the platform. "Another camper was stuck on the scramble web." She glanced up at the blackened canopy of branches above us. "Fast work, Bloom! You're getting to be as good at charms as your dad."

I felt a surge of pride. Being compared to Dad was high praise. He had once been the most powerful evil sorcerer on the planet. And now that he'd turned his back on the dark side and only used his magic for good, he was known as an exceptional wizard. I was really proud of him.

"Hey, where did that other kid go?" Hem asked, peering off into the trees. "He was the one who started the fire," she explained to Coach Clary.

"Oh, well, accidents happen," Coach Clary said. "I'm sure he didn't mean to cause trouble."

I was just about to tell her that the kid had also barged Benji off the course when Coach Clary clapped her hands to make the rain cloud drift away. Then she turned to Benji. "So, how are you enjoying the Charmed Ropes? I've noticed you're improving. You're going to do so well in the contest tomorrow."

Benji's glasses steamed up. "Um—thanks. Bloom is a great teacher."

"Oh, I don't know about that," I began, my face even hotter now.

"Benji is right," Coach Clary said, her eyes shining behind her hawk-goggles. "You're a very supportive team member, Bloom. Which is why I have a favor to ask. I have a new camper who is finding it hard to settle in. . . . I wondered whether either of you two," she said, looking at Benji and Hem, "might swap into another team so the new camper could be Bloom's teammate."

Hem and Benji looked at each other.

"I guess I don't mind," Benji mumbled, looking at his feet.

"Er—me neither," Hem muttered, her smile disappearing.

Coach Clary chuckled. "Let me see what I can do." She clicked her fingers and a clipboard appeared in front of her. "Ah, yes, this might work. . . . Hem, how about I put you on a team with your other bunkmates, Blush and Luna?"

Hem's face brightened. "Sure, they're fun."

Coach Clary scribbled the changes onto her clipboard. "Thank you, Hem. But make sure Blush and Luna don't use their wings." She laughed. "Fairies always seem to do very well in this contest. Now, how about you finish the course, and I'll meet you at the bottom of the zip line and introduce you to your new teammate."

As she flew off, I felt a slight wobble in my

tummy. I loved helping new kids settle in—as the owner's daughter, I felt that was one of my roles at camp. But after my recent experiences with my last bunkmate, Cruella, I also knew that it could be tricky.

"Ooh, I can see everything in the camp from up here," Benji said, peering over the edge of the platform. "Is that the Mystical Maze?"

"Yep, and there's the Dragon-Flying Course. You can see their fiery breath."

"Wow! I'd love to try that," Hem said.

Benji's eyes goggled. "Um—me too. I think!"

I laughed. "Come on, let's head for the zip line."

Benji reached for another flying feather and climbed aboard. "And this time I'm going to keep my eyes wide open," he said. "Because according to the book *Fifty Places to Feel the Heat Beneath Your Feet!* the zip line passes right over the top of the volcano."

Hem blinked at him. "I thought that was just a rumor."

"It's true," I said. "Dad told me it's buried deep underground and probably extinct. But sometimes I think I feel a little warmer near it. I'll show you."

This time Benji managed to fly in a straight line, and by the time we reached the zip-line platform, he was buzzing.

"I really feel I'm getting the hang of this now," he said, landing with a gentle bump. He laid his feather on the pile and picked up a zip wire grip. "Now I just need to make it down faster than last time."

"Me too," I told him. I usually went slow and steady. "Let's think fast thoughts."

He gave me a thumbs-up and then attached himself to the line and jumped, followed a moment later by Hem.

My turn. I fastened my grip to the cable and prepared to leap. This was my favorite part of the course; I loved the feeling of the wind in my hair when I whizzed down the line.

But as I stepped off the platform, it wasn't the wind making my hair stand on end. I could see Coach Clary and Benji waiting for me at the bottom. And next to them was our new teammate. . . .

"Oh no!" I gasped.

It was the blue-haired kid who had set the course on fire.

"BRAVO, Bloom!" Coach Clary called as I walked over to join them. "Lovely smooth zip lining! Come meet your new teammate." She smiled at the blue-haired kid. "This is Hades. Hades, meet Bloom. And you've already met Benji."

Benji looked at me, his eyes wide.

"Hi," I said to Hades. "Um—nice to meet you."

He nodded, glancing at Coach Clary and then quickly back to me again.

Maybe he thinks I'm going to tell on him, I thought. *And I probably should! Benji could have been hurt!* I didn't really want to be on a team with him.

"Coach Clary," Hades piped up. "Aren't there any other teams I could join?"

Huh? He seemed to be reading my mind. *Maybe he's good at that, just like Dad.* "No offense," he added, wafting his hand at me and Benji. "But see, they're not exactly the fastest kids on the course. And I've got a shot at winning tomorrow. Just not, you know, with them."

Benji's glasses turned strawberry red, matching his face. "Um, well," he muttered, looking down. "I wouldn't want to slow him down."

"Me neither," I said. *I want Hem back!*

Coach Clary frowned. "Winning isn't all about speed. You also need focus and the skill of being a good team player. Now, how about you guys get to know one another while I go hang these up?" She turned and scooped up a pile of ropes and headed toward the shed.

For a moment we all just stood there, staring at our feet. Then Benji coughed. . . .

"Um—so, you're an awesome feather flyer," he told Hades. "Do you practice a lot? I read about this kid who could ride upside down and do loop-the-loops faster than an actual griffin."

Hades gave a half smile. "You should try flying with a monster like Cetus chasing you."

Benji's eyes sparkled. "Cetus? Wait—that's

a sea serpent, right? I think there's something about him in my Awesome Creature Trading Cards. . . ." He began searching his pockets until he pulled out a bulging wallet. "A, B, C . . . Cetus! Yeah, here it is." He leaned in so Hades could look, too. "Did you know that sea serpents can live to be five thousand years old?"

I smiled. It was good to see Benji back to his chatty self. But I couldn't shake off the worry of being on a team with Hades. There was something so unpredictable about him. I looked across the yard and saw Coach Clary through the open shed door.

"Hey, Bloom." She looked up from the ropes

she was untangling as I walked inside. "Have you come to help?"

"Sure." I crouched down and started winding one of the cables.

"So I guess you're a little worried about Hades, right?"

I blinked at her. *Huh? Can Coach Clary read minds, too?*

"I know he can be grumpy," she went on. "And yes, he breaks the rules, too. But he's also passionate about magic. Just like you and Benji."

"Yeah, but he's a bit"—I tried to think of a polite word for Hades's bad attitude—"pushy?"

Coach Clary nodded. "There's a reason why he's like that. He has a brother who is really good at lots of activities. And Hades feels that nothing he does is ever as good as his brother. 'Sibling rivalry,' they call it. I used to feel a bit like that with my little sister, Sage." Coach Clary chuckled. "When we were young, she'd make such fabulous enchanted cakes, and I just burned everything."

I laughed. "But you're great at other things. You

were the fastest grown-up on the course when we had that campers-versus-counselors contest."

"Oh, that was fun," Coach Clary said. "And you're right, everyone has different skills. But the trouble is, Hades and his brother, Zeus, both like the same activities."

"Zeus?" I frowned. *That name sounds familiar.*

"He was here at camp a few summers ago. Do you remember him?"

"Wait! Was he the kid who liked thunderbolts?"

Coach Clary nodded. "I think there's a photo of him, somewhere." She walked over to the pin-board. As I joined her, we scanned the pictures of former campers.

"There!" she said, pointing to a picture.

"Oh, wow! Zeus won the Charmed Ropes Relay."

"In record time," Coach Clary said. "I'm guessing that's why Hades wants to win it, too. In his head he has to match what his brother did. Or better it."

I understood now. We had a lot of siblings at camp, and they were sometimes competitive with each other.

"That's why I want Hades to be on your team," Coach Clary added. "You are kind and supportive and you always follow the rules. That's exactly the example that Hades needs right now."

Just then we heard the sound of laughter from outside. . . .

As we poked our heads through the shed door, I saw Benji riding a feather around the yard with Hades chasing after him, waggling a brush.

"That's it," Hades was shouting. "Pretend I'm a fang-toothed giant sea serpent about to eat you for breakfast. Then you'll move faster."

Benji laughed so hard he toppled off.

"Aw, come on!" Hades groaned.

But Benji was giggling too much to catch up.

Coach Clary smiled. “I think Benji’s sweet nature will be good for Hades, too.”

I nodded. Benji’s enthusiasm was infectious, and it was nice to see him having a good time with Hades. *Maybe Coach Clary’s right,* I thought. *We just need to show Hades that being on a team can be fun—win or lose.*

"**SO**, what sort of things do you like to do?" I asked.

Me and Benji were giving Hades a tour of the camp, hoping we'd find somewhere we could practice our teamwork skills ahead of the ropes contest the next day.

Hades shrugged. "The usual stuff. Magical Combat. Bigfoot Wrestling. Chess with the Fates."

"The Fates?" Benji's eyes widened. "Aren't they the goddesses who plan what happens in your life?"

"Yep," Hades said. "They're powerful and crabby and you don't want to get on their bad side. But that's what makes it exciting."

I shivered. "Isn't there anything a little less risky?"

Hades stopped walking and thought for a

moment. "Flaming Archery? I smoke out the competition."

I glanced at his blue hair with the tiny fiery sparks at the tips. "Maybe I should introduce you to Sylvester," I said. "He likes that sort of thing. . . ."

"Really?" Hades suddenly looked interested. "Who's Sylvester?"

"He's one of the counselors," I explained. "A ghost who used to be in a magical circus. I've seen him do fire-eating and flame-juggling on talent night."

"Whoa!" Hades breathed. "That's more like it. Where do I sign up?"

"At Pinecone Point!" Benji said, hopping from foot to foot. "I've just checked today's schedule on my lenses—"

"Benji's got enchanted glasses," I explained to Hades.

Benji nodded shyly, tapping his magical frames. "And Sylvester is running circus classes today."

"What are we waiting for?" Hades said. "Let's scram!"

"Um—sure," I said. "Only, I don't think Sylvester will be teaching fire skills. Probably something less dangerous."

Hades's shoulders drooped a little. "What, you mean he'll be doing boring stuff like lion-taming? Or hammer-throwing? Or just lying on a bed of nails?"

"Er . . . well."

Hades sighed. "I guess it's better than nothing. Come on. I'll race you there."

By the time Benji and I panted our way up Hickory Ridge—the steep track that leads to Pinecone Point—Hades was already there, lounging against a tree.

"What took you so long?" he said smugly.

I was too puffed-out to reply. I collapsed on a boulder next to Benji as we caught our breath.

"You guys need to train," Hades said. "Personally, I run up Mount Olympus every day, so this place is as flat as a pancake to me."

For a moment I wondered if he'd cheated. *Maybe he found a shortcut. Or borrowed one of the counselor's Glow-Carts. Or used one of the secret underground tunnels...* I sighed. *Nah, don't be unkind, Bloom; he's just faster than you!*

"Come on," I said, standing up. "Let's go say hi to Sylvester."

I led them through the trees where the large circus tent was pitched. From inside we could hear the sound of piped organ music, and the sweet scent of cotton candy hung in the air.

Hades pushed past me to get inside.

"What in the underworld?" he muttered as he pulled back the door flap. "Where are the lions?"

THERE were no lions. But lots of exciting activities were dotted around the circus ring—hovering stilts, magical bubble balls you could ride inside, and an enchanted tightrope that kept changing. One moment it was a normal cable, the next it was a washing line, then a wriggly snake, then a jungle creeper with glowing lizards darting along it.

"Hey, check that out!" Benji pointed to a group of campers juggling with Mystery Eggs. My eyes widened. You didn't want to drop one of those; each one contained a secret spell! "Oh, and look up there!" Benji added, peering above our heads, where a group of kids were playing on a trapeze. "Are they actually flying?"

"Yeah!" I said. "Want to have a go?" I could see Glissando, one of my favorite counselors, working with them. She waved when she saw me.

But Benji was already distracted. "They're making balloon animals over there . . . and the animals are really alive."

I laughed as a poodle-dog balloon ran past, barking and wagging its tail.

"Oh, watch out!" Benji cried as a kid tumbled toward us, cartwheeling wildly. But just as we were about to dive out of the way, he vanished into thin air. "Walloping wands!" Benji muttered. "Where did he go?"

"It's Abracadabra Acrobatics," I explained. "Now you see them, now you don't!"

Hades snorted. "Balloon animals and handstands? Snooze fest. Where's the contest? Where's the risk? My grandma could do this stuff."

Huh? I wanted to point out that my granny Maj was a three-time gold-medal winner in the Extreme-Broomstick-Flying Olympics and she could probably outride Hades. But I didn't want to start a fight. *Remember, Bloom, you're trying to get him to be part of the team.* "There's Sylvester!" I said, changing the subject.

We headed across the ring, dodging acrobats, plate-spinners, and several kids swooping low on their flying unicycles. I noticed Hades start to frown—which deepened when a balloon snake nearly tripped him.

“Hello, Bloom!” Sylvester waved when he saw me. “And who have you brought to circus school?”

“Hi, Sylvester, these are my buddies Benji and Hades.”

“A pleasure to meet you.” Sylvester made a bow, which turned into a spectacular forward tumble followed by a backflip.

“Crashing cauldrons!” Benji muttered. “That was awesome.”

But Hades just sighed and folded his arms.

Sylvester smiled at him. "You look familiar. Have you been here before?"

"No."

"Do you perhaps have a family member at camp?" Sylvester peered at him more closely.

"No!" Hades snapped. "I've told you. I'm here by myself."

Sylvester shrugged. "Apologies . . . Now, I was just about to start my clowning-around class. Care to join?"

Hades shook his head. But Benji was nodding enthusiastically. "Ooh, yes, please! I read about this in the schedule," he added to Hades. "It's invisible clown magic you shake out of a tub, right?"

"Exactly!" Sylvester clapped his see-through hands, and a small blue container with little holes in one end appeared.

"A spell in a saltshaker?" Hades muttered. "Yawns-ville!"

Sylvester paid no attention to Hades. He turned the container upside down and began

scattering the invisible contents around our feet. "This is the best way to practice clowning. This spell creates invisible obstacles that will slow you down or knock you over or sometimes make you disappear altogether."

Benji let out a huge sneeze. "Sorry, magical allergies!"

Hades looked at the ground. "I don't see anything."

"Exactly," Sylvester said. "Try walking and you might *feel* something."

Benji's eyes sparkled. He pushed his glasses up his nose and took a big step. "Whoa!" he cried as his foot slipped and he jolted forward. "It's like walking on ice—wah!" He gasped as he zigzagged right, bumping into one of the plate-spinners. "Oops, sorry!" The plates smashed onto the floor but then instantly pinged back together.

"No problem," she said as her plates began to spin once more.

Benji's eyes boggled, then he sneezed again. "I love it here! Come on, Bloom, join in."

I hesitated for a moment. Clowning around wasn't usually my favorite activity. I never liked anything I couldn't control. But it was hard to resist Benji's enthusiasm. And after spending time with him I'd come to realize that sometimes being a little out of control could be fun.

"Okay, here goes . . ." I went to take a step, but something invisible pushed me back. "Hey! What's happening?" I tried to move again, leaning in with all my might, but then the force suddenly stopped, and I shot forward, nearly colliding with a passing balloon bear.

"Ha-ha!" Benji laughed. "That was so funny, Bloom."

I grinned. "I guess it was a little ridiculous."

Hades groaned. "This is so childish."

"Um—hello," I said as I hit a slippery section and nearly fell over. "We *are* children!"

Hades looked so disgusted, I couldn't help laughing. Benji joined in. And Sylvester chuckled, too.

"Why not have a go, Hades?" he suggested. "You might enjoy it."

"Thanks, but no thanks. I'm going back to the Charmed Ropes Course." But as he turned to leave, his feet stayed where they were. He tried to move them again. "What in the name of Olympus?"

"Oh, the spell must have spread," Sylvester said. "I think you've got treacle feet."

"Don't worry," Benji called, setting off toward him. "I'll pull you out—"

But just at that moment, Benji's feet seemed to hit a particularly slippery spot, and suddenly he was sliding out of control—straight for Hades!

"Stop!" Hades growled.

But Benji couldn't even slow down. There was a loud CLUNK as their heads collided.

Hades clenched his fists and flames shot out of the tips of his hair. One of them flew straight into the side of the tent, where it set the whole wall of canvas ablaze.

"Blistering broomsticks!" I cried. "Not again!"

SEVERAL campers squealed. A balloon popped. And the jugglers dropped their Mystery Eggs, releasing a smattering of sounds and smells and sparkles.

"D-d-don't w-w-worry," I cried, my hands trembling, my legs like jelly. "I'm a trained junior fire warden."

Before I could begin my extinguishing spell, Sylvester appeared, raising his hands to the scorching flames. *"Cherry soda, sweet and bubbly. Turn this danger to something lovely!"*

There was a cracking sound like a soda opening, followed by the smell of cherries, and instantly the fire vanished. The walls of the tent changed into an ice-cold igloo—glistening and iridescent.

"Sparkling spell socks!" I said. "How did you do that?"

"It's a switch spell," Sylvester explained. "Especially useful when you're dealing with powerful magic that you haven't got the strength to reverse—or just something dangerous like a fire." He turned to the rest of the campers. "No need to panic, everyone. And now it's snack time!"

At the sound of his words, a food wagon painted in pink and white candy stripes rolled inside the tent.

But I was too fascinated by the igloo to join the line now forming. I reached out and touched the tent's icy glow. My fingers tingled at the cold.

"Bloom! Did you see that spell?" Benji said as he came to stand next to me. "It was the coolest magic ever . . . literally!"

"Yeah! I'd love to try a switch spell sometime. Hey, have you seen Hades?" I dragged my eyes away from the shiny ice to look around.

"I think he's gone outside," Sylvester said, appearing next to us.

"I guess he feels bad for accidentally sparking that fire," Benji said.

Or maybe he just wanted to leave in case he got in trouble! I sighed, reminding myself to keep an open mind. "Yeah, I suppose he didn't mean to set the tent on fire. He just gets so frustrated when things aren't going his way."

Benji nodded. "I don't understand why he didn't like clowning around."

"He prefers competitive activities," I said. "See, he has this brother—"

"Zeus!" Sylvester cried. "I remember now. I have a memory for faces, you see."

"Wow! I didn't know he had a brother," Benji said. "Is he at camp, too?"

I shook my head. "He was here a few summers

ago. And he won every contest. That's why Hades is so competitive. He wants to match what his brother did."

Sylvester smiled. "My cousin and I were exactly the same. We used to haunt an old hotel together, and we'd always try to outdo one another with the number of guests we could scare."

"Really?" I couldn't imagine that. Sylvester was the least terrifying person in camp.

"Yep," Sylvester said. "We'd float through walls, or shake some rattly old chains up in the attic. Or just make the books in the hotel library pop out of their shelves!"

"Whoa, that does sound creepy," Benji said.

Sylvester nodded. "We were so busy competing with each other, we never stopped to think of how scary we might be. Once I even haunted a kid's birthday party and made the cake float across the room. . . ."

Benji's eyes goggled. "That sounds awesome!"

"His mom didn't think so," Sylvester said. "And neither did the kid when I accidentally dropped the cake!"

I shuddered at the thought of the mess. I didn't even like seeing cake crumbs on the counter.

"That's why I joined the enchanted circus," Sylvester said. "I wanted to make kids smile, not scare them. I learned to channel my energy in a new way."

"But Hades hates circus skills," Benji said.

"True, but there will be something else here at camp that he will enjoy," Sylvester said, bending down to pick up a balloon giraffe that was trotting past. "Something where he can use his quick mind and passion. He just needs to puzzle out what that might be."

Puzzle out? I blinked at Sylvester, an idea slowly forming in my mind. Something exciting and competitive but also an activity where we could work as a team? "Wait—that's it!" I said. "The Mystical Maze!"

"Ooh, I've read about that," Benji said. "It's the mysterious hedge puzzle, right? With lots of traps and dead-ends. And isn't there an awesome prize if you make it to the middle?"

"A magical Oracle Cap," I said. "Every camper who finishes the maze gets one. The cap can answer any yes-or-no questions."

Benji's glasses flashed with excitement. "I'd *love* one of those."

Sylvester's eyes twinkled. "Then I very much hope you win, Benji. Though if you do, make sure you're ready for its answers. In my experience, the truth isn't always easy to hear—even from a magical hat."

"YEAH, yeah, I get it, thanks." Hades yawned. "Stick to the paths. Don't go under or over the hedges. Watch out for traps. Can we start now?"

We were in the line waiting to enter the Mystical Maze, while Galen, the minotaur counselor who ran it, gave everyone instructions. Hades was standing on tiptoe, trying to peer over the hedges.

Though I wished he'd listen to Galen, it was good to see Hades so enthusiastic. Ever since I'd mentioned this idea, his sulky mood had lifted and he'd been much chattier.

"Blah, blah, blah!" Hades muttered as Galen continued. "I just want to get inside!"

"You should really pay attention," I whispered. "I've tried the maze loads of times, and I've never finished it."

Hades rolled his eyes. "My brother Zeus said it was easy—like taking candy from a baby cyclops."

"Did he win one of the caps?" Benji asked.

"Yeah. And if Zeus could do it, anyone can. Come on, let's make like a Pegasus and fly." Hades went to cut the line and pass the other campers, but Galen stepped in front of him.

"One moment—I still need to run through the safety tips."

"How hard can it be?"

Galen snorted, and a puff of hot hair blew out of his nostrils. "Don't underestimate the maze. It can be challenging. There are all sorts of obstacles like—"

"The Wheelie Centaurs!" Benji piped up. "They're these little people-ponies on wheels. If they tag you, you have to go back to the beginning."

"Correct," Galen said. "There are also—"

"The Scrunkles!" Benji burst out. "Little magical skunks that scuttle around silently, trying to spray you with sticky toffee sauce. If you get squirted, you get stuck until the spell wears off."

"Correct again," Galen said. "But there are other challenges, such as—"

"The moving hedges!" Benji gushed. "And the sliding trapdoors. And the secret passageways and, and . . . Oh, I'm so sorry," he added to Galen, his glasses turning bright red like his face. "I didn't mean to keep interrupting you. I'm excited."

Galen smiled patiently. "I understand. I still feel like that, and I get to play in the maze every day. It's good that you're so well informed."

"Oh yeah," Benji said. "I have read SO much about this place. I can't wait to see it all and—"

"And we definitely don't need to wait in the line," Hades interrupted. "Not with my friend here knowing so much." Hades took Benji's arm and tugged him toward the entrance. "You really should write a guidebook," he added to Benji, who beamed back. "You're like the Plato of puzzles!"

Galen looked like he was about to object, but just then one of the younger campers farther back in the line let out a cry.

"Nosebleed!" one of his friends shouted. "He was levitating upside down."

"Wait here," Galen said as he trotted off to help.

Hades seized his chance. "Quick, let's get inside while the minotaur's not looking."

"We can't!" I said. "Not without Galen's permission. The maze can be scary if you don't know what you're doing."

"But we do know what we're doing . . . at least one of us does." Hades gave Benji a big grin. "You'll help us, won't you, pal?"

"Um—sure," Benji said.

"Because we're a team, right?" Hades gave

Benji a thumbs-up. And Benji's glasses got foggy.

A team? I thought. *That's new!* Was Hades starting to realize that working with other people might be worth it after all?

"Come on, Bloom," Hades called from the gate. "We can't do it without you."

Me? I glanced back down the line, where Galen was still busy mopping up the little camper's nosebleed. Then I looked back at Hades and Benji, who were both now waving at me to follow them. I hesitated for a millisecond. . . .

If Hades is really starting to think of us as a team, I don't want to let him down. I stole another glance at Galen, then raced after them. *Broomsticks crossed that this isn't a Mount Olympus–size mistake!*

"SO which way?" Hades asked as we pushed through the turnstile.

Just inside the gate, the hedge puzzle split off in three different directions. Each one looked the same.

"Um—I don't think it matters," Benji said. "I've read lots about solving mazes and you just have to keep your right hand on the hedge at all times, then you'll eventually find your way to the middle."

Hades shrugged. "Okay. But just so you know, we have to make it there in fifteen minutes."

"What?" I blinked at him. "That's impossible."

"My brother did it in sixteen," Hades said, "and we've got a leg up with our dream team here. Anyone got a timer?"

"Me!" Benji fiddled with his magical glasses, and a little ticking clock appeared on the side of the frames. "Ready?" he asked as he set it to zero.

I nodded. But Hades was already dashing down the middle entrance to the maze.

"Keep your hand on that hedge, Benji!" he called back. "I'm depending on you. Because teamwork makes the dream work, right, guys?"

"Er—sure thing," Benji said as we followed. "I won't let you down."

I gulped. I've always been a little nervous of the maze. Mostly because you never knew what was about to jump out. The hedges towered, creating so many dark, shadowy corners where creatures could lurk unseen. . . .

"I hope the wheelie-centaurs don't tag us," I

whispered to Benji. "I really don't want to have to go right back to the beginning."

"Me neither," he said. "If we do, there's no way Hades will beat his brother's time, and I want to help him. We're a team now, Bloom."

"Um—yeah, I guess." The path veered to the right, and the hedge split in two directions.

"Which way now?" Hades said, pausing for us to catch up.

"Um—maybe take the right-hand path," Benji said, his hand still on the hedge next to him.

"Wait! What's that noise?" I glanced behind us.

"Uh-oh," Benji murmured. "It sounds like wheels!"

"Run!" Hades shouted.

As we zoomed around the next bend, I looked back and saw one of the little pony-people in the distance, waggling his arms in the air, ready to tag us. "Faster!" I yelled to Benji and Hades. But Hades seemed to be slowing down.

"I'm just a little burned out," he panted, dropping back. "You guys keep running. I'll catch up."

That's odd, I thought, *he didn't get out of puff running to the circus tent!*

I carried on around the next corner, but when Hades didn't follow, I stopped. *This isn't what teammates do. We need to go back and face the wheelie-centaurs with him.* I was about to call to Benji, when my nose began to twitch.

Huh? It smelled like burning. *Oh no! Maybe Hades accidentally set the hedge on fire!* "Benji?" I said. But he was too far ahead to hear me. This was another reason I disliked the maze. It was easy to lose people.

The smell was getting stronger, so I retraced my steps to check on Hades. But as I turned the corner—"Hades?" He was dashing toward me. Behind him was a wall of thick dark smoke blocking the path where he'd been. "Crashing cauldrons!" I muttered. "Is there a fire back there?"

"Nah," Hades said as he ran past. "Looks like someone just made a smoke cloud. Lucky for us, eh? It should stop those roller derbies from catching up!"

Huh? Had Hades created the smoke? But just then Benji came running from the other direction.

"Stop!" he yelled. "There are Scrunkles up ahead!"

My heart thumped in my chest. I'd been caught by those little furry critters before. And it had taken nearly an hour for their sticky toffee spell to wear off. "We'll have to go back the way we came," I said. "The smoke's starting to clear now," I added, glancing at Hades.

"Nah. We can't go back," he said. "We'll lose time. We just need to make like the Trojans and go to war! Can't we just squish the Scrunkles?"

"No!" I said. "They're living creatures!"

We glared at each other as the seconds ticked away on Benji's glasses. Then Hades turned to the hedge and began patting it like he was looking for something. "Nope. No secret passageways in this section. Oh, well, I guess I'll just head over it."

"That's cheating!"

Before he could reply, there was the sound of footsteps running toward us, and three younger campers appeared through the drifting remains of the smoke wall.

As they got closer, I opened my mouth to warn them about the Scrunkles, but Hades drowned me out with a yelp.

"Cramp!" he shouted, hopping from one foot to the other. "Ooh! . . . Ahh! . . . It's in my leg. . . . Ow!"

"Oh, that can be so painful," Benji said. "I got a cramp once after using a swimming spell."

"Is he okay?" one of the campers asked. She was a small girl with fairy wings on her back. "Should we go find someone?"

"I'm fine," Hades said. "You guys just keep going," he added, waving them on. "I'll sing! That always makes it go away. *'Five giant fiery snakes,'"* he sang, *"'sat by a boiling lake. . . .'"*

The campers looked at one another, then shrugged. "Okay, bye, then," the fairy girl said.

"No! Wait!" I called as they jogged off. "There are Scrunkles up ahead. Don't go that way."

But they couldn't hear me over Hades's loud song.

"Oh, that's better," he said as soon as they were out of sight.

I didn't answer. I was waiting for the campers to reappear after they'd spotted the Scrunkles. But they didn't.

Hades did a few knee bends and leg stretches, then turned and grinned at me and Benji, his eyes gleaming. "Those critters must be gone by now. Let's move it."

Benji nodded. "I guess those kids would have come back if the Scrunkles were still lurking."

But as we turned the next corner . . .

"Suffering spells!" I muttered. "They got them!"

THE little group of younger campers was stuck fast.

"We got Scrunkled!" the fairy girl said, trying to move her feet from the toffee puddle they were stuck in.

"I'm so sorry," I said. *If only I'd shouted louder.*

"Do you think the spell will wear off soon?" one of the other kids asked me, looking at his sticky sneakers glued to the ground.

"Um—"

"Come on, team!" Hades jogged past. "We've

got to keep moving. According to your glasses, Benji, we've got less than seven minutes."

As he spoke, the hedge next to us suddenly vanished and a new one appeared, covered in brightly colored flower buds.

Benji sneezed. "Uh-oh. I think something magical is happening. It's making my allergies tickle."

"All the more reason to RUN!" Hades turned and raced down the path.

"The spell should wear off soon," I said, waving to the campers. "But holler if you need help!"

As we jogged after Hades, I couldn't take my eyes off the buds that were appearing around us. "See how they're wiggling and jiggling?" I whispered to Benji.

"Yeah, it looks like they're about to—"

POP!

Their petals unfurled and tiny little yellow butterflies shot out from inside, flapping around our heads.

"So cute!" Benji said, peering at them through his glasses.

But I wasn't so sure. Something about the bugs seemed familiar. . . . And then I remembered. "They're flutter-butter-byes!"

"Flutter-what-er-byes? Hey!" Benji cried as one of the butterflies lobbed a shiny dollop at his glasses. And then another. And another.

And suddenly they were all flicking slippery yellow globules at us.

"It's butter!" I called to Benji. "Careful not to slip on it."

The flutter-butter-byes were everywhere now, raining down their gooey glop on us.

I shuddered; I've always hated getting covered in slippery stuff.

"I can't see!" Benji groaned as it smeared over his lenses.

"Come on," I said, "We'd better get out of here." I grabbed his hand, and heads down, we charged down the path with the cloud of yellow beasties fluttering after us.

As we dashed around the next corner, I spotted Hades. *Wait—is he levitating?* Through the storm of butter balls, I was sure I saw Hades floating in the air, peering over the hedge puzzle. But my view was suddenly blocked, as a butter patty hit me in the eye.

"Yow!" I cried, wiping it off. When I looked again, Hades was back on the ground.

"Need some bug spray?" Without waiting for an answer, he clenched his fist, then tossed a ball of smoke our way.

"Duck!" I told Benji. We threw ourselves on the ground. When I looked up, the smoke had gone . . . and so had the butterflies.

"Neat trick!" Benji said, standing up and wiping the butter off his glasses. "Thanks for helping."

"Well, we're a team, aren't we?" Hades said. "And 'team' stands for: Together Everyone Achieves More."

"Awesome!" Benji's eyes were shining now.

I nodded. "Yeah, er—thanks." I thought about the smoke cloud from earlier. I wanted to tell Hades that smoke clouds weren't allowed in the maze, but it felt ungrateful.

"And good news," Hades added. "I think we're close to the end now."

Yeah, I thought, *because you just peeped!*

"Come on, let's run the rest of the way—oh, wait!" Hades suddenly froze as though he was listening to something. "Did you hear that? Someone's shouting for help!"

"I don't hear anything," I said.

Hades ignored me. "Maybe I should climb over the hedge and check they're okay."

"That's not allowed," I said.

"But what if someone is hurt?" Benji said. "Maybe they fell."

Hades nodded. "That happened to me in a labyrinth when I was little. I broke my leg. It was next-level scary."

"Really?" I looked at him. It did not sound like Hades. *He's usually boasting.... Maybe he really did hear someone shout.* I thought about the campers who'd been Scrunkled. "We'd better go look for Galen."

"That'll take too long!" Hades said. He glanced at Benji. *Was he just checking the clock on Benji's glasses?* "Maybe there's another way to get through the maze . . . you know, to help the camper in distress," Hades said. "Benji, could your glasses see if there's a secret passageway nearby?"

"Um—maybe," Benji said, tapping the frames.

"Don't do it, Benji!" I said. "It's cheating!"

"It's not," Hades scowled at me. "I checked the rules before we came in. And there was NOTHING that said you couldn't use magical glasses. And don't forget, you're allowed to use the secret passageways if you find them. Galen said so."

Benji nodded. "I guess if it's helping someone who's hurt, it would be okay. Right, Bloom?"

I tried to think of what Dad would say. *He would tell me to put people first, rules second.* "Okay," I said. "If you really think someone is in danger."

Benji was already scanning the hedge. "There!" he said, pointing to the bottom. "I can see door hinges."

Hades reached out and gave the section of hedge a shove. It instantly swung open. "Let's rock and roll!" he called, diving through the gap.

I felt a wobble in my tummy. *This just doesn't feel right.* But Benji was already halfway through the door.

Was I really going to break the rules? After all, we hadn't just stumbled upon the doorway. But if Hades was right, and someone really needed us, then— "I'm coming!" I called as I ran through. *Broomsticks crossed, this is the right thing.*

"CONGRATULATIONS! You beat the maze!"

Huh? I blinked through the bright lights coming from the booth in front of us. Inside, I could see Tarragon the faun, one of the counselors who helped Galen run the hedge puzzle.

"Bloom! Can you believe it!" Benji cried. "We uncovered the secret door to the center!"

Sure, I thought as I scrambled to my feet, *because Hades floated over the hedge to spot it.*

"Hey, Bloom." Tarragon waved to me from his booth. "You guys are the first team to find the hidden doorway this summer."

"And in record time," Hades said, pointing to the clock on Benji's glasses. "Fifteen minutes and thirty-five seconds."

"That's an outstanding time," Tarragon said. "Very nearly a course record."

Hades's smile vanished. "Very nearly?"

"Oh yeah, we had this kid a few summers ago who managed it in fifteen minutes, twenty seconds," Tarragon said, pointing to a wooden pinboard on the front of his booth. "You'll see his picture there."

Hades leaned in to look. "Zeus!" he hissed, and little sparks shot out of his hair. "*Of course* he rounded up."

"But don't worry," Tarragon said, "I think you're likely to win THIS summer's course record, so be sure to add your names to the leaderboard. Here—" he said, offering Hades a quill pen. "Now, what color caps would you like?"

While Benji chose his Oracle Cap, I waited in line behind Hades. "So, where's the person who needed our help?" I asked.

"What? Oh, I don't know. I must have misheard." He shrugged distractedly. "Or maybe I got the direction wrong. Or someone else helped them first."

Or maybe you just made it up!

"Look, Bloom!" Benji said, holding up his green cap. "This is the coolest thing, ever. . . ." He put it on.

"Did I have prickle pickles for breakfast?" He took it off and peered at the front. "See? It says 'no,' which is true! I had waffles, as always."

"That's great," I said. But I had a bad taste in my mouth, and it had nothing to do with the thought of prickle pickles.

Hades had picked his cap now and slunk past me, clutching an orange one. But he didn't even glance at it.

I suddenly felt a little sorry for him. *It must be tough to be always trying to outdo your brother.*

Especially if you don't even enjoy the prize at the end.

"And what color cap would you like, Bloom?" Tarragon asked.

"Oh—um—any of them is fine, thanks."

"How about *sky-spell blue*? I bet you can't wait to show your dad," he added. "He'll be so proud of you."

I tried to smile and nod. But I felt a little cloud of guilt hovering above me. *Maybe I shouldn't take it,* I thought. I was still wavering, when something small and silver whizzed past my head, landing on the counter of the booth.

"Flashing feathers!" Benji cried. "Is that a clockwork carrier pigeon?"

Tarragon nodded. "The counselors use them to chat with one another around the maze."

He took a little folded scroll from the bird's beak and unraveled it.

"Oh dear," he said. "It seems that one of the campers has fallen and sprained her ankle."

I felt my cheeks burn, realizing there *had* been someone calling for help after all. I watched as Benji called to Hades to walk back with us. Had I been wrong about our new teammate? Had he genuinely thought he was going to help someone?

But I saw him floating! I reminded myself. *AND he blocked that Wheelie Centaur with smoke. . . . But then again, he also used that smoke to help us with the butterflies. Or was that just to make sure we got to the middle quicker?*

I sighed.

The maze wasn't the only puzzle today.

11

AS we headed back, I wished I could talk to Benji about Hades. But they were chatting about the ropes contest the next day. Hades seemed to have gotten a second wind.

"If you want to win, you need to 'Go big or go *Homer*!'" Hades explained. "It's all or nothing!"

Benji nodded enthusiastically.

"Just break the course down in your head," Hades continued. "The first part is like a kindergarten play zone; it's just platforms and walkways. . . . Then there's the scramble web. Move fast and the spiders won't get you."

"Really?" Benji said.

"It's a case of 'You snooze, you lose!'"

"But what about the moving climbing wall?" Benji asked.

"Just make like a lizard!" Hades mimed himself

scaling an invisible wall. "Lean in. Bend your arms and tell yourself you've got sticky hands."

"Whoa, that's an awesome idea," Benji said, copying Hades's moves.

"I know we're going to smoke out the others tomorrow," Hades said. "We'll break all the records."

"Do you really think so?" Benji pushed his glasses up his nose. "I've never won anything before . . . well, apart from this cap."

"Of course we'll win!" Hades said. "You'll be awesome. After all, you've got more brains than the Hydra . . . and that's a lot of heads!"

Benji giggled.

"You should take up Magical Combat," Hades went on. "Trust me, when someone's casting stinging spells at you, you learn to move a lot quicker."

"But don't stinging spells hurt?" Benji asked.

"You don't get hit if you move fast enough," Hades said. "Plus, you use a shield spell. Then magic bounces off you."

"Ooh, I've read about shield spells. I'd love to

try one sometime. . . ." He bounced on his heels. "Hey! you should check out the camp's Museum of Mythical Objects. There's this awesome shield that's made out of raindrops."

"Raindrop shield, you say!" Hades's eyes sparkled. "This I gotta see."

"Um—I don't know . . ." I said. Being around Hades was a little exhausting.

"Can't we, Bloom?" Benji asked. "There's time before dinner. And I know Hades would love it."

It was hard to say no to Benji. "Okay. Let's go."

The Museum of Mythical Objects was my dad's latest project. As a former evil sorcerer, he had a large collection of enchanted things. Everything from spell swords to a giant flying suit of armor with metal wings and a pair of shoes that gave you rocket speed. My favorite piece was the phantom coat. When you wore it, you could walk through walls just like Sylvester!

"The museum's in here," I said as I led them up the steps to the large cabin where Dad kept his collection.

"Towering Titans!" Hades breathed. He looked around at the hundreds of glass cabinets. "This place is awesome."

I felt my chest puff up with pride.

"Wait until you see the Lightning Hammer," Benji said. "It makes real thunderbolts. Mr. Maj demonstrated it last week. Oh, and I've got to show you Orion's Belt—it's made of actual stars, and then there's the—"

"What's this?" Hades interrupted, peering into a long, low cabinet just inside the door. "It looks like a model of the camp?"

"Oh yeah, check out the volcano," Benji said. "See, it lies just below the Charmed Ropes Course."

"A real volcano?" Hades asked.

"Don't worry," I said. "Dad says it's probably extinct."

But Hades had already moved on to the next case and was pressing his nose against the glass. "What's that?"

"That's Mr. Maj's sorcerer's staff," Benji whispered, his voice full of awe. "Some say it's THE most powerful magical conductor ever known."

Hades's eyes widened. "Really?"

"Yeah, but Dad doesn't use it now," I said quickly.

"I wish I could give it a spin," Hades said, patting the glass as if he was looking for the opening.

"Sorry. The case is locked." *Broomsticks crossed! That staff is WAY too dangerous.*

"Hey, didn't you want to see the raindrop spell shield?" I asked. Something about the way he was looking at the staff made me a little uneasy.

But Hades didn't move. "It looks like a plain old wooden stick," he said. "Except that knot at the top is shaped like an eye. I swear it's staring at me."

"Maybe it is," Benji said. "According to this book I read about Bloom's dad . . ." He looked at me as he spoke, and his glasses steamed up. "This staff was carved from the wood of the Dragon's Eye Tree."

"No wonder it's so powerful," Hades murmured.

I shivered. I'd never liked Dad's old magical staff much. But Hades seemed spellbound.

Before I could say anything, there was a sudden blast of cold air. Benji sneezed. Both doors of the museum burst open, and a giant black stallion thundered into the room.

"Watch out!" I yelled as we dived out of the way.

12

"**WHAT** in the name of Mount Olympus . . . ?" Hades cried as the horse reared up onto its back legs, puffing plumes of green smoke out of its nostrils.

Benji's eyeballs were like dinner plates. But I wasn't worried. There was something familiar about the horse's kind eyes. . . .

"Dad!" I breathed.

And a heartbeat later, the horse vanished and my father stood in its place. He winked at me. "Apologies for the alarm," he said, bowing to Benji and Hades.

"Alarm? What alarm? Consider me un-alarmed," Hades mumbled, picking himself up off the floor and shaking the carpet fluff off his clothes.

Benji grinned. "Awesome, Mr. Maj!"

"Thank you, Benji. Sometimes we all need to feel the wind in our manes as we gallop across the sky, don't you think?"

Benji's glasses glowed. "Um—yeah, definitely."

"Welcome," Dad added, looking at Hades. Then he smiled at me. "Hello, Bloom, are you having a good day?"

I tried not to meet his gaze. Dad could read minds, and I didn't want to bother him with my concerns about Hades. He always believed in giving people the benefit of the doubt; as a former evil sorcerer, he knew exactly what it was like to have people mistrust you.

"Well . . . It's been a puzzling day," I said vaguely.

"Ah yes, the Mystical Maze," Dad said.

"Huh! How did you know?"

"The cap." Dad pointed to my head.

I reached up and groaned. I'd forgotten I was wearing it. I quickly took it off.

But Dad didn't ask any questions. "I'm glad you're here," he told me. "I'm about to set up a new display. Perhaps you can help me for a moment."

I left the boys to look around the museum and followed Dad to the other end of the room, where a wooden box was sitting on a table.

"Go ahead," he said. "Take a look inside."

I leaned in. "Musical instruments?"

"Magical musical instruments!" Dad reached inside and took out a little wooden flute covered in dust and cobwebs. "You've heard of the Pied Piper, I think."

"Wait! Is that his pipe?"

Dad smiled.

"But it looks so small and . . . ordinary?"

"Sometimes the things that appear small and ordinary are the most powerful, like this shell."

Dad plucked a tiny pink conch out of the box. "It doesn't look very important, but if you blow through it, you can summon a kraken, one of the fiercest sea creatures you'll ever meet."

"I hope I don't meet one!" I wasn't the strongest spell-swimmer at camp, mostly because I didn't trust water magic. It was always so unpredictable. I peered into the box again. "A ukulele!" I pulled out a small guitar with weather pictures painted on the front.

As I began to strum, little rainbows appeared, dancing around me.

"I won that at sorcery school when I was very small," Dad said. "My brother and I both wanted it. . . . You know how competitive we once were."

I tried not to laugh. "You still are!" I thought of all the family dinners when Dad and his brother, Uncle Mel, would try to outdo one another with spells. Dad would start with something small, like making the cutlery dance, then Uncle Mel would join in by turning the napkins into real birds. Then Dad would enchant the water glasses into sparkling fountains, and Uncle Mel would turn the fountains into ice sculptures. It would go on and on until Granny Maj got fed up and told them to stop.

"Well, yes, perhaps." Dad chuckled. "But you know, Bloom, a little bit of sibling rivalry is actually quite healthy. It helped make Uncle Mel and me better at magic. When one of us learned to do one spell, the other would teach himself something even more exciting."

I nodded. Sometimes I wished I had brothers and sisters, but being an only child meant I didn't need to share the limelight with anyone. I thought of Hades. Sibling rivalry didn't seem to bring him any joy.

"You and Uncle Mel are both powerful magicians," I said. "But what if one of you had been a little worse at spells?" I looked down the room, where Benji and Hades were now playing enchanted chess on one of Dad's special sets—the one where the little pieces are real mini prehistoric beasts.

"Yes, I see your point," Dad said. "But it can also help with determination."

I guess that's true. I remembered how enthusiastic Hades had been in the maze. He'd never once thought about giving up.

"It's just about finding a way to channel that competitive passion into something positive," Dad said.

Maybe that's how I can help Hades, I thought. *By finding some activity that isn't just about winning.* I was about to ask Dad if he had any ideas, when there was a loud shout from the other end of the room.

"Argh!" Hades fumed. "I can't believe you put me in checkmate!" Tiny sparks flew out of his hair as he picked up the woolly mammoth and tossed it aside.

The little chess piece let out a shriek. But in the blink of an eye, Dad appeared by Hades's side, catching the mammoth in his hand.

For a second I wondered if Hades would be in trouble. But Dad just took the ruffled little chess piece and replaced it on the board. "Come," he said, beckoning us to follow him. "Let me show you something."

He walked over to the case that contained his old magical staff.

"It's easy to get annoyed when things don't go our way," Dad said, looking at Hades.

Hades shuffled a little and didn't meet Dad's eye.

"In the past, I often used this staff to take out my frustrations," Dad went on. "I remember losing a flying contest at a wizards' convention, and I used it to spark an earthquake."

Benji's eyes looked like they were out on stalks. "No way!"

"Really?" Hades said. "The staff can do that?"

"Thankfully, an older and wiser wizard stepped in and reversed the spell before it could cause any damage." Dad sighed. "I later learned that it is better to use magic to build than to destroy."

A thoughtful look passed over Hades's face. But it was hard to read what he was thinking.

"Learn to channel your drive, Hades," Dad said. "To help others, if you can . . . And now, I think you'd all better run, or you'll miss dinner."

As we headed for the door, I thought about what Dad had said, about how Hades should find a way to help others. And then an idea popped into my head. *Perfect!* I thought. *I just need to find Glissando.*

13

"**WHAT?** You want ME to help out with the camper games tonight?" Hades scowled. "Why?"

"Um—because it's a great way to get to know people," I said. *Plus, if you're* setting up *the games for the other campers to play, then you won't be so focused on winning!*

We'd just finished dinner (my favorite: potluck pie, in which the ingredients magically changed with every bite), and we were sitting on the grassy banks outside the Cozy Cauldron Café.

"But I don't want to get to know other people." Hades folded his arms. "I'm happy hanging out with my teammates. Right, buddy?" he added, winking at Benji, who beamed back.

"It'll be fun," I said. "And besides, I already told Glissando we'd do it."

"I'll help!" Benji said, hopping from foot to foot. "I know this awesome game called Flip the Pancake. You'd really like it, Hades."

"There's Glissando!" I said, waving to a counselor with a purple ponytail who was carrying a clipboard.

Glissando was one of the kindest counselors at camp. She was so relaxed, she seemed to glide when she moved.

"Hey, Bloom! Hey, Benji, and this must be Hades," Glissando said. "Nice to meet you."

Hades nodded but didn't say anything.

"Benji was just telling us about an awesome game," I said.

Glissando smiled. "Sounds great! What equipment do we need for it, Benji?"

"Um—just a few blankets."

"No problem!" Glissando slipped a small golden pencil out of her pocket and began drawing in the air.

Benji's eyes grew wider as a rectangular

shape began to appear, then—"Achoo!" He sneezed as a neat pile of folded purple blankets tumbled to the ground. "But how . . . ?"

"Enchanted pencil!" Glissando said, holding it out for him to see. "So useful! All you need to do is think about what you're drawing, and the picture comes alive. Now let me gather a few of the campers, and we'll get started."

Hades stalked off to go sit on an old log on the far side of the grass. But as the campers began to line up and Benji started to outline the rules, I noticed Hades was listening.

"So—um, if you could all please—er . . . climb on these pancakes," Benji told the kids.

"I think Benji means go stand on the blankets," I explained.

Benji's face turned pink, and so did his glasses. "Exactly, thanks, Bloom. The blankets are supposed to be like giant pancakes—now stand close together, about six or seven of you on each pancake."

Hades was watching now, his brows knitted together with concentration.

"So all you have to do is try to flip your pancake—your blanket!—over," Benji said, "without anyone falling off, or putting a foot on the ground."

The kids looked at each other and giggled.

"Wait!" Hades jumped to his feet. "Why don't we have team leaders? I'll take this group," he said, squishing onto the first blanket.

"Er—okay," I said, moving to another one. It was good to see Hades getting involved, but *we* weren't supposed to be *playing* the games. I glanced at Glissando, but she nodded back encouragingly.

"Okay, team," Hades said to the other campers on his blanket. "Let's talk tactics—everyone huddle—and keep your voices down," he whispered. "We don't want to help the others!"

I groaned. *Why does he always have to be so competitive?*

But there was no time to argue. Glissando had already blown the whistle and the game had begun.

This is so hard, I thought as me and my teammates flailed around, trying to tug one corner of our blanket over without tipping everyone off. Kids wobbled. Elbows went in eyes. And someone tumbled off altogether. Then one of the younger kids nudged me.

"Look!" he said, pointing to Hades's blanket. "Are they allowed to do that?"

I glanced across and my eyes goggled. Hades and his team were floating above the ground while one kid remained on the blanket to turn it over.

"Hey!" I cried. "That's cheating!"

"No one said you couldn't use magic!" Hades said.

"He's right, Bloom," Benji called from somewhere under a mound of arms and legs and heads. "I forgot to say that bit."

"And DONE!" Hades yelled as his team's blanket flipped over, and they all landed with a bump. "We won! What's the next game?"

I sighed. *I guess that was kind of clever. . . . And, whoa! His teammates look so happy.*

"Hades is awesome," I heard Benji murmur to the kids on his blanket. "He really thinks outside the magic box."

I tried not to laugh. That sounded exactly like something Hades would say. *But Benji's right. Maybe Hades's love of sports isn't such a bad thing. . . .*

AN hour later, after Hades and his team had won nearly every game and Hades had spent the evening boasting about how we were going to scorch the ropes course in the morning, I suddenly realized he'd vanished. I looked around at the groups playing abracadabra board games, magic ball, and the ones on the enchanted drawing table with Glissando. But he wasn't with any of them.

"Have you seen Hades?" I asked Benji, who was sketching a shell-covered shield with one of the magical pencils.

He stopped drawing and blinked at me from behind his glasses. "Maybe he went to bed already?"

"Nah, he would have walked past to get to the bunks."

Benji looked around. "I don't see him, but—hey, there's Sylvester!" He waved to the ghost who had suddenly appeared, but Sylvester was talking to one of the counselors. He looked even paler than normal and had a serious look on his face. The counselor shook her head, and Sylvester's shoulders seemed to droop.

"Come on," I said. "Hey, Sylvester!" I called as we crossed the grass toward him.

The ghost was rummaging in the picnic trash can now. He looked up and smiled as we approached, though his eyes didn't sparkle as usual.

"Have you lost something?" I asked.

He nodded. "One of the circus spells has gone missing. The clowning-around spell in that shaker, remember?"

"Sure," I said. "The one that made the invisible obstacles."

Sylvester went back to rummaging. "I thought someone might have thrown it away by mistake," he said. He moved a chocolate banana skin and some vanishing-candy wrappers, and peeped underneath. "Nope, nothing." He sighed. "I guess

I'd better go find your dad, Bloom. The spell can be a little unsafe if you're not expecting it, and I wouldn't want any campers to have an accident."

As we watched him go, a sudden thought flashed into my head. Did Hades take the shaker? It seemed such a coincidence that he went missing at the same time the spell had vanished. . . . *But why?* Hades hated the circus skills class.

"Maybe we should look for Hades," I said. "It's nearly bedtime. . . ."

Benji nodded. "We all need a good night's sleep if we're going to smash the ropes course tomorrow. I really don't want to let Hades down."

"Sure." But I knew I could have Sleeping Beauty levels of shut-eye and still not be the fastest on the course. And I had a weird feeling in the pit of my stomach. For the next hour or so, we searched the camp for Hades, until the light began to fade.

"Maybe we should borrow one of those?" Benji suggested as a Glow-Cart whizzed past us.

It was tempting. The little Glow-Carts were used by the counselors to get around. They were strictly off-limits to campers, but Benji and I had borrowed one before when we'd had to rescue a rare magical creature. "I wish we knew which direction he took," I said. "If you were Hades, where would you go?"

"The Charmed Ropes Course!" Benji said without thinking. "Oh!" he gasped, covering his mouth with his hand. "Why didn't I think of that before?"

I smiled. "Dad says we sometimes don't see what's right in front of us. Though I think he was talking about my Aunt Belladonna; it's hard to see her because she's a phantom. Come on . . . let's head over to the ropes."

It was nearly dark by the time I slipped the bolt on the gate leading into the course.

"We'd better be quiet," I whispered. "Campers are not allowed in here at night."

"In case they fall?" Benji asked.

"Yeah, and also because the woodland night creatures like to take their turn on the course." I shivered. Some of the nocturnal beasties were a little spooky.

We headed down the pathway. The climbing walls and wooden structures cast creepy shadows. I was glad Benji's glasses had begun to glow, illuminating the way.

"Whoa," he whispered, glancing up at the trees. "They look even taller at night."

I suddenly felt cold. "Maybe we should go back to the bunks. Hades is probably there already."

"Good plan," Benji whispered.

But as we turned, I heard a twig snap behind me. "What was that?" I spun around. "Hades?" I peered into the gloom, but I couldn't see anything. Then I heard a low growling noise from the other direction. *Uh-oh!*

"Quick!" I hissed to Benji. "RUN!"

WE dashed back toward the gate, but just as we reached it, a blur of blue shot out in front of us.

"Hey, B and B. Where's the fire?" Hades demanded, the fiery tips of his hair glowing in the darkness. "Are you following me?"

"What? No!" I said, catching my breath. "But we were trying to *find* you. It's nearly bedtime. And besides, you're not allowed here after dark."

Hades rolled his eyes. "I just wanted to get some extra drills in before tomorrow." He looked at Benji. "Because we're going to light up the contest, right?"

Benji smiled. "Oh, sure."

"Practice makes perfect and all that—especially if we want to win," Hades continued.

I peered at him. *If he really wanted to practice, why didn't he ask me and Benji to join him?*

Hades turned to look at something. I followed

his gaze—the Enchanted Ropes Wall of Merit. And at the top of the board was Zeus. I sighed. *I guess it must be hard to see your brother's name everywhere you look.*

Benji had noticed, too. "Couldn't we just have a quick run?" he whispered to me. "I really want to help Hades win tomorrow . . . but I could use some practice."

"Me too," I said. "But it's so dark now."

We looked back at Hades, who was still standing in front of the board. His head was down and his shoulders were all slouchy. "So long, dreams," I heard him murmur. "It would have been fun to have had a chance."

Benji looked at me with pleading eyes. "Please, Bloom. We've got to help him. . . ." Suddenly his face lit up and his glasses glowed brighter. "I know! We just need some headlamps. And I can make them." He pulled one of the enchanted pencils from his pocket. "I accidentally put this in my pocket when we left to look for Hades."

I nodded. Headlamps were a good idea. Though as Benji got to work doodling them, I couldn't shake off the worry. I hated breaking rules. *But we're a team!* I reminded myself. *Maybe this will help us all work together better. Teamwork takes practice, too.*

"Okay!" I called to Hades. "We'll run the course with you. But just for ten minutes."

I expected him to look pleased, but he was already setting off. "Fine! Just try to keep up."

The first section of the enchanted ropes was fairly easy. It began with a climb up a tree ladder, which led to a low platform. With our headlamps to light the way, it was easy to find the handholds. I noticed Hades had already zoomed off in front.

All I could see of him now was the flashlight bobbing about in the darkness and the faint glow of his blue hair. *Whoa, Hades really is good at the course.* Watching him zooming along made me want to move faster, too.

"I can't wait to take on the scramble web again," Benji said as he pulled himself up onto the first platform. "Hades says the best way to avoid the spiders is to run superfast! Come on, Bloom, let's go!"

Head down and glasses glowing, he charged off along the narrow walkways.

I took a deep breath and ran after him. I wasn't usually a huge fan of the scramble web—especially not in the dark—but watching Hades and Benji getting into it seemed to have lit a spark in me.

I raced forward, stopping next to Benji in front of the gleaming web. It was exceptionally springy. One wrong bounce and you'd jump right off. Plus, it was the home to a family of giant pink Stink Spiders. Trust me, you did not want to let one of those critters get too close—they squirted a pong-cloud that smelled like rotten cabbage.

Benji didn't looked worried. "Here I go!" he called, diving onto the web.

It was hard to see much in the gloom. But then—

"Made it!" I heard Benji shout from the other side. "Your turn, Bloom!"

Okay, here goes! My heart began to beat faster.

I was more than halfway across when I heard it—a yell from somewhere in the darkness. I stopped and listened. Then I heard it again. It sounded more angry than scared.

"I think it's Hades," Benji shouted from the other side of the web. "Oh, watch that spider, Bloom!"

I turned my head and spotted it just in time, scuttling toward me with its pink pong-cloud fangs raised. I threw myself into a forward roll and dived onto the platform next to Benji.

"Made it!" I panted.

But Benji was staring into the darkness. His lenses had popped out like little telescopes.

"Uh-oh," he murmured. "Hades is surrounded!"

"**SURROUNDED** by what?" I asked. There could be anything lurking on the ropes course at night. Naughty goblins. Pesky prank elves. Or a whole host of bothersome beasties like—

"Fire-breathing dragon-squirrels!" Benji gasped. "I've never seen them before. But I've got an Awesome Creature Trading Card about them somewhere. . . ." He began patting his pockets.

"Show me later," I said. "We've got to go help." I wasn't actually worried about the squirrels attacking Hades; I was more concerned about what HE might do! *If the squirrels AND Hades get angry, we could have a two-way fire battle on our hands!*

We raced across the next few obstacles—a moving climbing wall, followed by the floating log-circle stepping-stones, and then on to the aerial tunnel that twisted and turned as we crawled through it.

I spotted Hades as soon as I poked my head out the other end. He was on the next platform, facing a semicircle of cranky-looking squirrels, their luminous green fur glowing in the dark.

"Hades!" I called. "Don't move. We're coming. . . ."

"I've got it, I've got it," he snapped.

As he spoke, the squirrels banged their tails against the floor.

"Uh-oh! They're getting mad," I called. "You should leave."

"No way!" Hades glared at the squirrels. "Move it fluff-balls, coming through."

But as he stepped toward them, they let out a hissing sound, and tiny flames shot out of their nostrils. Then they reached down and picked up handfuls of acorns and hurled them at him.

"Hey!" Hades yelped as the little missiles pinged off his head. "That stings!"

He leaped toward them, but the little squirrels dived for the trees and kept pinging him with acorns. The fiery sparks of his hair were growing larger now.

"Benji!" I called. "We've got to stop this before Hades sets that tree on fire. Maybe we could scare the squirrels away?"

"Ooh—I've got an idea." Benji pulled out the magic pencil from his pocket and began drawing in the air.

"What is that?" I asked, staring at the strange shape he was doodling.

"It's an ice-breathing, squirrel-chasing tabby cat!" Benji said proudly as the creature he had drawn plopped heavily onto the platform.

About three times the size of an ordinary cat, it had long orange whiskers, only one ear, and a huge tail shaped like a tennis racket.

"I'm not so good at drawing tails," Benji whispered. "You can tell it's a cat, right?"

The creature let out a low, gravelly meow and a cloud of icy dust shot out of its mouth. It set off, thudding down the gangplank. . . .

I held my breath as it brushed past me, but it had its eye on the squirrels.

"Flying Furies!" Hades muttered as it plodded toward him. "What is that thing?"

Before Benji could explain, the cat lunged for the tree, sending the squirrels scattering off in all directions.

"It worked!" Benji cried.

"That's great," I said. "But who's going to catch the cat?" The furry creature was sitting in the tree now, licking its jumbo paws.

Benji giggled. "Don't worry. Glissando says the stuff you draw only lasts a little while. It should vanish soon."

Broomsticks crossed! I thought.

"Okay, guys," I called. "It's getting late. We should get back, otherwise the counselors will look for us. Come on, there's an emergency ladder off this platform."

Hades hesitated for a moment, then nodded. "After you."

But just before we reached the bottom, Hades

shouted from above. "I must have dropped my sundial watch. I'll go back and get it."

We waited for him by the gate. We waited. And waited. I checked the little clock on Benji's frames again. "It's been twenty minutes. Do you think he ran into the squirrels again?"

"Maybe the cat got him!" Benji laughed, then saw my face and stopped. "It's okay, Bloom, I drew it so it only chases squirrels, not campers!"

I checked the time again. "We're going to be in so much trouble—"

"Don't get your tunic in a twist!" Hades said, suddenly appearing from the darkness.

"At last!" I felt my shoulders relax a little. "Did you find your watch?"

"Nah, I just remembered I didn't put it on this morning. Race you back!" he called as he disappeared into the night.

THE competitors were already lining up by the time me, Benji, and Hades arrived at the course the next day. I waved to a couple of the counselors who were helping organize the contest. I'd always loved competition days. Not because I ever won anything, but there was always such a buzz around camp. Kids were chatting excitedly together in groups, munching high-energy sparkle-snacks, and checking that their laces were tight, while the counselors ticked off their names on clipboards and handed out magical timer wristbands.

"Wow! There are so many teams," Benji said, his eyes wide.

"Yeah, but they don't stand a chance," Hades said.

Really? I couldn't work out how he could be so confident. *Loads of these kids will be great at climbing,* I thought. *It's not as though we've got a secret plan to make us go faster!*

Hades was doing some leg stretches and knee bends now. Benji joined in, too.

"Tell me the rules again," he asked, hopping from foot to foot. "I'm so nervous I've got brain fog."

"It's easy," Hades said. "The three fastest teams in round one go through to the final. And that means us. Because we're the dream team, right, guys? After all, we've got your brains, Benji . . ."

"Thank you!" Benji's face turned red.

"And your good sense, Bloom," Hades continued.

"Er—thanks."

"And my ultimate warrior skills. And together we're the A-Team, that's 'A' for 'absolutely one hundred percent awesome,'" he added, winking at us.

I saw the determination in his eyes, and suddenly I felt a surge of motivation, too. *Maybe he's right,* I thought. *Perhaps we just need to believe we can do it, and we will. . . .*

"Next team, please!" Coach Clary beckoned us toward the gate. "Morning, guys. Looking forward to the race?"

"Of course!" Hades answered. "We're going to take the cup, right, team?" He looked at me and Benji.

"Definitely!" Benji said, giving him a thumbs-up.

"Sure!" I found myself saying.

Coach Clary's eyes twinkled. "Okay, well, here are your wristbands. They will automatically start timing you as soon as you start to climb. And there's no point in one person racing off."

She looked at Hades. "You ALL need to make it to the other end, so make sure you support one another. Oh, and if you fall off, you go back to the beginning and start again."

As we headed down the path to the start of the course, Hades suddenly leaned in close to me and Benji. "Stay to the left-hand side," he whispered. "I noticed a few hazards last night, but they're mostly on the right of the course. Good thing we practiced, huh?"

I blinked at him. "What hazards?"

But Hades had already launched himself onto the first ladder. "See you on the other side," he called as he shimmied up and disappeared onto the first obstacle.

"**BENJI**, wait!" I called. "What did he mean about hazards?"

"Er—maybe there are some loose boards, or—um—slippery leaves, or acorns?"

"But Coach Clary always flies around the course before a contest," I said. "She'd have removed leaves or acorns or—"

"We can ask Hades later," Benji called as he pulled his Oracle Cap on and reached for the ladder. "Come on, let's go!"

I gave him a few moments to reach the first platform, then I began to climb, too. But I couldn't shake off the bad feeling that had returned to my belly. And it had nothing to do with the giggle-berry waffles I'd wolfed down on the way to the competition.

Whoa! My foot hit something slippery as I pulled myself onto the first platform, and I stumbled forward, nearly tumbling onto the safety net below. I steadied myself, peering down to see what had tripped me. *That's weird . . . I don't see anything.* I set off again, but a few footsteps farther along—*uh!* My right foot hit something sticky, and I floundered on the spot.

"Frosted fairies!" I muttered, trying to pull myself out of what felt like an invisible patch of glue. I yanked my foot free and set off again, only this time I kept to the left-hand side. *Hades is right,* I thought, *there are no hazards over here.*

Up ahead, I could see Benji diving swiftly across the left side of the scramble web. But

others weren't so lucky. Several campers looked like they were stuck. One was holding her nose.

"I've been ponged!" she groaned.

And they weren't the only kids having problems. I looked around the rest of the course and saw some campers falling off the obstacles, and others were tripping over invisible blocks. Lots were waiting to be rescued from the safety nets below. And a bunch of the flying feathers seemed to be whizzing around in the air by themselves, like a flock of badly behaved birds.

Something strange was happening. *But what?*

I carried on, hugging the left side of the course. And apart from an odd gust of strange, sudden wind that nearly blew me off the stepping-stones and a section of the zigzag-zone beams where I forgot to keep left and nearly tumbled over, I managed to reach the flying feathers.

Benji was just ahead of me. He waved, but then— "Achoo! Achoo! Achoo!" He took off his Oracle Cap and pulled out a big purple hanky to wipe his eyes. "My allergies are going nuts!" he shouted. He sneezed twice more and then set off on the final zip wire.

A few minutes later, I whizzed down to join him. Hades was waiting for us at the bottom.

"Check out the scoreboard!" he said, a huge smile on his face. "We're in the lead."

I glanced at the giant, floating scroll hovering over the course. "Wow, that's—um, amazing."

"I guess all that practice worked," Benji said before he sneezed again. He blew his nose.

"Maybe the flying feather magic set you off," I said. "It's a powerful charm."

Benji nodded. "But it wasn't just that section. I've been sneezing all the way around the course." He wiped his runny eyes behind his glasses. "Oh, and you were right about those hazards, Hades," Benji added. "It felt like the whole course had been covered with Sylvester's clowning-around spell!"

Huh? I stared at Benji, suddenly feeling cold;

the type of cold you get when someone conjures up a big, dark rain spell that blocks out the sun on a summer's day. *Sylvester's clowning-around spell? The one that went missing last night?* I glanced at Hades, but he was watching with a grin as the other competitors finished the course. My mouth suddenly felt dry.

HAD Hades really taken the clowning spell and scattered it on the course? That's what it looked like. But accusing him of such major cheating without proof made me feel all squishy inside. *What would Dad do?*

I remembered something he'd once told me. We'd been on the beach doing sand-spells together, turning sand sculptures into creatures. I'd made a cute crab with wings and a rainbow shell, and as it scuttled off sideways into the sea, Dad said we could learn a lot from crabs. They were clever because they didn't tackle things head-on like a bull, which could make a situation worse, but from the side.

Okay, Bloom, I told myself, *make like a crab. . . .*

"So, Hades," I said. "Thanks for the warning about the course."

"You're welcome," he said, his eyes glued to the scoreboard.

"You spotted the new obstacles last night, right?"

"Yeah." Hades shrugged. "Maybe those squirrels made them."

That made no sense at all! I looked at Benji, but he was sneezing some more and didn't seem to have heard. "So maybe we should go tell Coach Clary," I said. "Then the counselors can clean up the course to help the other competitors."

"What?" Hades spun around.

"And we should probably also ask to have some time added to our score," I said. "Because we knew about the hazards, but the other competitors didn't."

"No way!" Hades glared at me. "That could mean we'd miss the final! Just because we put in extra practice doesn't mean we should be punished. Anyone could have found them if they'd bothered to take the time to look."

Before I could reply, there was a loud cheer as another team finished with a strong time.

Hades glanced up at the leaderboard. "Ha!" he muttered. "They didn't beat us."

"It's Hem's team," Benji said, waving to her, Luna, and Blush as they walked past. "Hey, guys, well done."

"Yeah, congratulations," I called, feeling a wave of relief at seeing another team manage to finish the course. "How was it?" I said as I went over to talk to them.

"So tricky," Luna said, shaking out her wings.

"Yeah, I nearly fell off three times," Blush added. "Look, I scraped my knees!"

Hem nodded. "It was so much harder than yesterday. There was this super-slippery bit on the zigzag beams—I skidded off and had to cling on."

I looked back at Hades. He was in a huddle with Benji now, whispering.

I said good-bye to the girls just as Hades started heading in the other direction. "Hey, wait up," I called. But he ran off. I looked at Benji. "Where's he going?"

"Just said he had to get something. I still can't believe we made it through to the final, can you?"

"I can!" I said, my eyes narrowing. "I think Hades may have cheated."

"What?" Benji's red, watery eyes goggled behind his glasses. "How?"

"Sylvester's missing clowning spell! Remember that it vanished last night? You said yourself that those hazards on the course felt exactly like it."

"Yeah, but—"

"And we found Hades at the ropes course," I added. "He could have sprinkled it around the obstacles."

"But we'd have noticed last night."

"Not necessarily," I said. "Remember Hades

went back onto the course to get his watch. . . ."

"B-b-but Hades wouldn't do that. We did well on the course because, like he said, we practiced. A lot! And Hades helped me get so much better, what with all his advice and encouragement. . . ." He took his cap off and ran his fingers through his hair. "I just can't believe he'd cheat." Benji started twirling his hat in his hands.

An idea popped into my head. "Why don't you ask your Oracle Cap?"

"Huh?"

"The cap," I repeated gently. "Maybe we can ask it if Hades cheated."

Benji looked down at his hands, then nodded. "Oracle Cap: Did Hades cheat in the enchanted ropes contest?"

I saw the answer flash up on the front of Benji's cap. And suddenly I remembered what Sylvester had said about the Oracle Caps. . . . How sometimes you had to prepare yourself for answers you might not like.

BENJI stared at the YES on the front of his cap and groaned. His shoulders drooped and he looked close to tears.

"I'm sorry, Benji. We should probably go tell Coach Clary."

Benji puffed out his cheeks. "This means we've broken the rules to reach the final. What are we going to do?"

"Maybe we could withdraw from the contest?" I said before glancing at his crestfallen face. "But first, why don't we to talk to Hades? See if there's some sort of explanation." I looked around the course. "I wonder what's taking him so long."

I looked back at Benji and saw he was biting his lip. "Bloom, Hades asked me what would happen if something canceled the contest before the final round."

"Canceled? What do you mean?"

"Like if an earthquake struck or a tornado appeared," Benji said. "He was so impressed when I could tell him exactly what the rules say . . . that whoever is at the top of the leaderboard after the first round would automatically win."

"But we're not going to have a tornado or an earthquake."

"I know," Benji said. "Only . . . Hades looked happy when I told him."

"Come on," I said. "We've got to find him."

We scouted around the edge of the course where the campers and counselors were sitting in groups chatting and eating snacks before the final. But there was no sign of Hades. I was just about to suggest that we go talk to Coach Clary after all when I spotted a flash of blue shimmying up the ladder at the start of the course.

"There he is! Hades!" I shouted.

Our teammate had reached the first platform now and was bounding along the walkway.

"HADES!" I yelled louder.

"What's that strapped to his back?" Benji asked.

I squinted in the sunlight to see. It was something long and thin wrapped in a dark cloth. "Some sort of stick?" I suggested.

Benji peered up through his magical glasses and quickly turned them to the X-ray setting. "It's your dad's sorcerer's staff!"

Uh-oh! My tummy felt like it was doing a flip-flop forward roll in Sylvester's circus class. "Wait! Remember that Dad told Hades about how he once started an earthquake with it?"

Benji turned to look at me, his face ghostly white, his glasses glowing warning-red. "You don't think—"

"Quick!" I said, racing toward the first ladder.

I ducked under the safety rope that had been strung across the ladder while the competitors and counselors took a break and scrambled up to the first platform, with Benji close behind. We raced along the first few walkways, but I could see Hades was already across the scramble web and heading for the higher platforms.

"We've got to catch up!" I called to Benji as we dived onto the scramble web.

All the extra practice had actually made us much speedier, and we both zoomed across to the other side before the Stink Spiders had time to notice us. We charged on, crossing several more obstacles, and making it over the moving climbing wall and the stepping-stones in no time.

We'd just crossed the zigzag beams and had set off on our first flying feather journey when Hades reached the highest platform, the one where the zip line began. He had his back to us, his arms outstretched with the staff in his right hand.

As we arrived at his platform, a low rumble of thunder sounded around the course, and a sudden lightning bolt cracked above Hades's head.

"What's he doing?" Benji whispered.

Just then, the course began to shake. I grabbed hold of the safety rope while Benji hugged one of the wooden posts.

"Is he spelling an earthquake?" Benji gasped.

I shook my head, my legs swiftly turning to jelly. "Look down there," I said, pointing to a cloud of hot smoke that had begun to rise from the ground below us. "I think he's lighting up the volcano!"

THE whole course was shaking now. Beams creaked. Ladders groaned. And the branches of the trees around us rattled and crashed against one another, their leaves whooshing as a strange, hot wind began to swirl.

"Quick," I whispered to Benji. "We've got to stop him!"

But Hades spun around, spotting us. "Go away!" he yelled. "I'm not losing!" He curled his left hand into a fist and shook a large smoke ball at us.

I put my hands up to try and waft it away, but Benji darted in front, holding on to his glasses and muttering under his breath. . . .

"Stones and iron, strong, hard shells. Create a shield and deflect all spells!"

As he spoke, the smoke bounced off his glasses and was swept away by the wind. Benji sneezed, then grinned at me.

"Wow! A shield-spell enchantment?" I said. "Awesome work!"

"I got the idea from Hades. I've been practicing—" But Benji's words were drowned out by a horrible splitting sound from far below us, and a blast of scorching air rushed upward.

"It's erupting!" Benji yelled, peering over the side to look. He turned back and his face was bright red and wet with sweat, his glasses steamed up.

"Hades! I yelled. "You've got to stop, NOW!"

"No way! If the contest is canceled, we win!"

"Not if you've cheated," I said.

Hades stuck out his tongue. "But no one is ever going to forget me! I'll be the camp legend instead of Zeus!"

Before I could reply, there was a loud explosion and a volley of hot rocks shot up from below. They crashed around the course, hissing and spitting and leaving red-hot marks where they landed. A few bounced onto the platform around Benji and me. We moved to kick them off, but one hit a rope close by. . . .

"It's on fire!" Benji gasped.

"D-d-don't worry," I said. "I'll do the extinguishing spell."

Hades snorted. "You're wasting your time. Your magic is too puny to compete with this!" He waggled Dad's staff at us.

I gritted my teeth. *I have to try! "Raindrops, rivers, and creeks full of trout,"* I shouted, *"send me a cloud and put this fire out!"*

There was a tiny, damp PHUT sound. And then—nothing. Benji didn't even sneeze! The rope continued to burn.

"What are we going to do?" I cried, looking at Benji.

"I don't know, Bloom," he said, his voice small and wobbly. "I'm not sure we can reverse his spell. It's just too strong."

But as he spoke, an idea began to form in my head. "Maybe we don't need to reverse it," I said slowly. "Maybe we just need to change it!"

"Huh?"

"Sylvester's switch spell! Remember how he said it was useful when you're dealing with powerful magic that you can't reverse? If we say it together, the magic will be even stronger."

I leaned into the heat from the volcano, raising my hands toward the scorching lava down below. . . . "Ready?" I called to Benji.

"Um—I just hope I can get it right, Bloom."

"You will. I believe in you. Besides, *we're* still a team."

We said the words together: *"Cherry soda, sweet and bubbly. Turn this danger to something lovely!"*

Hades let out a yelp. "NOOOO!" he bellowed. But it was too late.

Benji sneezed. And there was a cracking sound, like a soda bottle opening, followed by the delicious smell of cherries. Instantly, the heat, the noise, the horrible smoke vanished. The burning rocks that were shooting up toward us turned into—

"Candy?" Benji cried, his eyes out on stalks as little pink and yellow sugary treats landed on the platform. "Tumbling trolls!"

Down below there came a gushing sound. I poked my head over the side of the platform and saw the lava had turned into a fountain of lemonade. Little droplets were shooting up into the sky and raining down on us.

"Arghhh!" Hades yelled, wiping the drink out of his eyes. "I won't let you ruin this!" Flames shot out of his hair and he held Dad's staff up. . . .

22

BENJI coughed. "Um—sorry, Hades, but I think your staff has turned into a candy cane."

"What?" Hades did a double take at the pink-and-white stick in his hand. "In the name of the underworld!" He threw it to the ground and

kicked it. Then he grabbed a zip-line grip from the pile, his shoulders hunched now, the flames from his hair damp from the sticky rain. "I've had it with this place," he muttered. He jumped onto the zip line and vanished out of sight.

Benji picked up the candy-cane staff. "Do you think it'll stay like this forever?"

"I hope so," said a deep voice behind us.

I spun around. "Dad!"

He smiled down at me, his cape billowing in the breeze. "You were both very brave. Thank you."

Benji's face turned strawberry red. So did his glasses. "Um—it was nothing."

I wanted to confess everything. About what happened at the maze. And Sylvester's missing spell. Our secret nighttime practice session on the ropes course. And just how our team had got to the top of the leaderboard in the first round.

But Dad turned to the volcano and waved his hands, speaking softly under his breath. Instantly, the flying candy rocks and the lemonade lava stopped. I heard a low rumbling noise like a dragon with tummy troubles, and watched as the ground began to shake once more. But this time it was the sound of the volcano retreating into the earth.

"I'll take that," he said, reaching for the candy-cane staff.

"Will you change it back?" Benji asked.

Dad's eyes twinkled. "No. I much prefer it like this. Far safer. And now I must go and help tidy up so the final can start. I am looking forward to watching your team."

"But we can't—" I began.

"Of course you can," Dad said. "You and Benji deserve your place in the final, though I doubt your teammate will be joining you. I think he needs a little time to cool off."

That's for sure! I thought.

Dad sighed. "I hope one day Hades will learn to celebrate his own strengths instead of competing with his brother. Only then will he be truly happy."

A little while later, after Dad and the counselors had swept away the clowning spell and the candy from across the course and cleared off the sticky lemonade lava with a clean-up spell, the final began.

Of course, we didn't win the contest. We didn't even come second! But as we stepped up to receive our third-place rosettes, our legs weary and our puff all gone, we felt glad we'd finished the course together.

"Congratulations, Benji," Coach Clary said, handing him his rosette. "Your climbing skills have really improved."

"Oh—er, thanks," he mumbled, looking at his feet.

"It must have been all that extra practice." She smiled. "It's a shame Hades couldn't compete with you. Apparently, he had to go home. He felt a little sick after eating too much volcano candy."

Me and Benji looked at each other. Hades could certainly spin a yarn!

Benji was a little quiet as we left the ropes course. Then—

"I'm sorry I didn't notice what Hades was up to," he blurted out. "I was a little too quick to believe his stories, and I got caught up in the fun of being on his team." He bowed his head and sighed. "I guess he made me feel sort of . . . special. Like I had useful talents."

"But you do!" I said.

Benji looked up. "You think?"

"Of course! You're the one who realized the hazards on the course seemed like the missing clowning spell. And you made that amazing shield spell. Not to mention the fact that your help made the reversal spell work on the volcano." Benji perked up as I went on.

"And you know, I enjoyed being in Hades's team, too. Maybe not all of the time," I added, looking around at the giant piles of candy that still littered the edges of the course. "But working with him made me realize that success is a lot like making a really good magic potion. You need different ingredients: teamwork, focus, and competitiveness! But the balance has to be right."

Benji nodded. "I'm much better on the ropes course after all the help from Hades—only, I'm not sure that being the best at something is the most important thing." He stopped walking and took off his Oracle Cap, then looked around for a moment. "Hey, you guys!" he called to a group of younger campers. "Would you like this?" He held out his cap to them.

Their eyes goggled. "Is that a real Oracle Cap?" one asked.

Benji nodded. "Go ahead, take it."

"You can have mine, too!" I said, taking my cap off and handing it over.

We looked at each other and grinned as the group ran off, chatting excitedly.

"So, I was thinking," I said, linking my arm through Benji's. "How about we go get some practice in before tonight's camper games?"

"Huh?"

"Well, see, my team completely flunked the Flip-the-Pancake blanket game last night," I said.

Benji chuckled.

"But I've got loads of ideas for next time," I said. "I think the recipe for success in *that* game is: a pinch of extra practice, a dose of determination, and a large scoop of teamwork—"

"And a big dollop of magic—and syrup," Benji added. "I'm in! Only, this time can we be on the same team?"

"Always," I agreed, "because as someone recently told me: teamwork makes the dream work!"